IN EVERY WAVE

Charles Quimper

IN EVERY WAVE

Translated from the French by
Guil Lefebvre

QC FICTION

Revision: Katherine Hastings, Peter McCambridge
Proofreading: David Warriner, Riteba McCallum
Book design: Folio infographie
Cover & logo: Maison 1608 by Solisco
Fiction editor: Peter McCambridge

ISBN 978-1-77186-155-7 pbk; 978-1-77186-156-4 epub;
978-1-77186-157-1 pdf; 978-1-77186-158-8 mobi/pocket

Artwork on page 7 by Nadia Saad. From an original series of ink drawings inspired by this novel.

Legal Deposit, 4th quarter 2018
Bibliothèque et Archives nationales du Québec
Library and Archives Canada

Published by QC Fiction
6977, rue Lacroix
Montréal, Québec H4E 2V4
Telephone: 514 808-8504

QC@QCfiction.com
www.QCfiction.com

QC Fiction is an imprint of Baraka Books.

Printed and bound in Québec

Trade Distribution & Returns
Canada and the United States
Independent Publishers Group
1-800-888-4741
orders@ipgbook.com

We acknowledge the financial support of the Société de développement des entreprises culturelles (SODEC), the Government of Québec tax credit for book publishing administered by SODEC, the Government of Canada, and the Canada Council for the Arts.

Funded by the Government of Canada
Financé par le gouvernement du Canada | Canada

Conseil des Arts   Canada Council
du Canada   for the Arts

Société
de développement
des entreprises
culturelles
Québec

IT WAS JUNE when I set sail on my boat's maiden voyage. I carried the bare essentials. A few pounds of supplies, your little pink box, a battle-ships game, and the endless echo of our days together.

The pink box held your collection of moonstones.

She may not look like much, but my new boat is the best friend I've ever had. We sail the world together looking for clues, signs, traces of you.

I cling to your name like a man desperate and dispossessed, probing the sound as it emerges from my mouth into silent starless nights. I ponder it from every angle, whisper it, recite it like a poem or prayer. I hiss it like a threat.

However intoned or inflected, your name remains unchanged, always ending on the same note that lingers in the dark, like the inkling of a ghost.

Beatrice. Your mother and I chose to name you Beatrice.

My voice has changed and it keeps catching me off guard. It isn't mine anymore. It isn't even a voice anymore. More like the rasping, creaking sound of a raven or locust. Or maybe an out-of-tune banjo. I can't decide which.

Another notch in the mast with my pocket-knife. One more day without you. Water covers everything, and its ebb and flow set each day's rhythm, sometimes raging, sometimes indolent, sometimes sad. As time passes, somewhere deep beneath the surface, the ocean's belly swells with a rumbling, palpable electric charge. I can sense a storm coming as well as any sailor, and I brace for it.

A BIRD GLIDES OVERHEAD. Could be a cormorant. Maybe an albatross. Might be just a seagull. I have no idea.

It's there first thing in the morning and follows me all day, circling above, tracking me across the seven seas.

Cracked skin, calloused hands. My body sculpted by the sea.

The steady rhythm of the galley inside me. Turmoil and rain-filled sorrow. A hint of something sweet, clear, and amber. A mournful melody. I think of you every day, seeking your shadow in the boat's wake, finding nothing but the sea.

I whisper your name softly on crisp September mornings and hold it tight against my chest on windy days. It's a confession and a plea. A lullaby for the fish.

I left you behind, my love, but I'm the one drowning every day.

::

Watching the bird soar above, one hand on my lower back, the other shielding my eyes. Long minutes pass. From time to time the bird dives under and comes up clasping a fish. So I rouse myself. Put the nets out, bait the lines, and wait. The sea feeds me, the skies quench my thirst. Seasons pass, and time washes over me like November rain.

Sprawled out on deck, watching ripples form on the surface of the water. I imagine the surging waves they are destined to become. Maybe these waves will reach you. The rising sun finds me at last. The sea spray clings to my eyelashes and falls in tiny droplets to the deck. I finger each one, desperate but determined to find a hint leading to you.

Every drop offers hope. Like a heatwave leaves you praying for rain. Like spring offers the promise of a thaw.

::

Did you learn about the water cycle? Every drop of water on the planet follows a well-defined order. From every stream, river, lake, and deep blue sea it rises unseen into the sky, falls as rain or snow or sleet, and swells the waterways once again.

Every body of water is drawn to the sea. That's all I know for certain. It's what keeps me going. Maybe I can track the current that carried you away. Maybe it will lead me to you.

I am a dying star, a fading supernova, but there is strength yet in my hands and somewhere in my chest. If I search long enough, I'll find you. It's inevitable.

DO YOU REMEMBER our holidays on Neptune? We spent every summer there, splashing around in the clear river. Pure and clean as holy water, it flowed around us. Mom would sit under a tree, lost in her reading, a castaway washed up on the pages of her book. You would pretend you were a sea lion or a submarine, and my laughter would echo in the forest. We used blue fern, petrified wood, and sheet metal from our rocket ship to build a shelter against the high winds.

The whole universe was our playground, and we explored its furthest reaches every Sunday after bath time.

We would play Marco Polo by the Great Dark Spot. The wind was so strong you could hardly put one foot in front of the other. One of us would hide in the methane clouds while the other searched blindfolded, hands out and trying not to stumble.

I'm almost positive I heard you fall that day, babygirl. I think I heard a splash.

THAT DAY.

I seem to recall your sandals had disappeared. We searched the tent, then gave up and let you go barefoot.

Maybe you slipped away under the low boughs. Were you following some little critter or a shiny bug? Or were you just too eager to go swimming?

I would have sworn you were helping Mom collect twigs for kindling. I'm sure I caught a glimpse of you two through the trees.

I think I spotted a blood-red cardinal in a mountain ash and figured we could get a closer look. I must have gone back to the tent for my big binoculars.

Where were you in that instant? Already struggling in the dark at the bottom of the river? Still safely at your mother's side?

I searched for you for hours. I screamed so loud and so long the echo still recalls my cries with a shudder. I looked behind every rock and in every bush until the only possible answer was the river. Everything inside me went quiet, and the horror crept into my bones. Was I careless? Did I abandon you? Panicked and alone in the water with no one to help you?

The police and their dive team never found you. They spent days in their boats, probing the riverbed with long poles but they couldn't find a trace. Had you already reached the ocean?

The next day's paper ran a paragraph about a tragic accident, a momentary distraction with fatal consequences.

::

You can't have just evaporated, dissipated into the atmosphere that blazing hot day.

All I remember is the sound of something breaking inside me and flooding everything. You were wildfire, an avalanche, a hurricane.

Something's been bothering me, and the more I think about it the more certain I am that your coffin was empty.

::

My body is a bitter lagoon, a still heart beneath a hundred fathoms of water, a shipwreck lying among eels and seaweed.

I've discovered a breach on my temple, hidden under my hair. I think you might be seeping out of me from there. I clap my hand to my head and try to plug the leak, but you keep slipping out. You mustn't wander off, sweetie. Stay close to Daddy. He doesn't want you to get lost.

Every day I sit on the deck of my boat and write to you. Every day I set my memories down on the wrinkled, stained pages of my logbook so I don't forget them, so I can keep them close. My memories are gradually fading, eroded by the steady sea breeze. It's getting harder to keep them organized, in logical order. Inside me the tide is slowly grinding you into sand.

::

At the helm on a sea tinted purple like wine. The horizon swallows the sun and swells in tawny-coloured hues. If you saw me now, you'd probably laugh at Daddy the Sailor Man. Or you might be scared, like that Halloween when you didn't recognize me in my costume. You ran from me, and I had to approach you slowly, carefully, like a frightened animal, before you let me pick you up and make everything alright again.

My hands are covered in stitches. One for every grain of sand in my hair and maybe then some. I tend to each cut with fishing line and a barbless hook.

Every morning brings the icy dew carried by the sea wind. I get up, shivering, toss the nets overboard, and bait the lines with yesterday's scraps of fish.

Frost on the deck. I scrape it up with my knife and melt it for drinking water in the midday sun. I season my meals with the salt that encrusts the sides of the boat as the seawater evaporates.

I'm scared. What if I don't recognize you? What if I pass right by you one morning without really seeing you? What if you've grown too much during all this time at sea?

You went under, and I've been at sea ever since, searching for you in every wave.

I promise, sweetie. I'll never take my eyes off you again.

::

The princess and the pea. That was you. You loved vanilla ice cream, summer rain, and the green caterpillars with blue spots that lived in the trees in our backyard. You loved sparkly stickers, cereal box prizes, and birthday banners.

You had oatmeal with maple syrup for breakfast every morning. You hated wearing your yellow raincoat and your big rubber boots. They made you trip over your feet when you searched for snails or fed chickadees in the yard.

You loved it when I came home from work with a little white stone I'd taken from the rock garden at the mall. You would hold it like it really had fallen to Earth from the moon just for you. You would run upstairs and put it in the pink box with the others. The one I gave you on your first day at daycare. The one that comforted you after a big storm blew down an oak tree in the neighbour's yard across the street. A moonstone for when Grandpa died. Another when you banged your head on the coffee table and it bled. A moonstone for every tear. You used to say the moon was magic, that it healed scraped knees, sprained ankles, chickenpox, and vaccination jabs.

::

Maybe there's a place where everything lost at sea winds up. I could pick you up at the flotsam and jetsam counter. A city beneath the waves populated by drowned sailors. An underwater cathedral covered in shells. Sea cucumbers growing in watery fields. A marketplace selling plankton and kelp, golden shrimp and sea lettuce by the pound.

I close my eyes and imagine your little body drifting in the current. I hope the water is warm. I picture your hair floating like silk around your head and brushing lightly against your shoulders.

When I try to imagine your companions, I think of squid and fluorescent sea dragons and pretty little fish by the hundred.

I can only hope there are other children there. And coloured pearls. And coral.

On calm evenings, I sometimes drop anchor near shore, where I'm lulled by the melody of cannibal urchins, sabre-toothed shellfish, and electric sardines. Sometimes I sit on the beach, bury my feet in the sand, and watch a slow procession of fish cruise by, the sound of the waves a soothing accompaniment.

I think of you every night before falling asleep.

I imagine you sleeping soundly, curled up on your side.

In your pink bedroom, breathing in, breathing out.

: :

The last news I had of you was in the calm, dark waters of the North Sea. I found a flash of lightning trapped in a droplet clinging to my net.

I freed it very carefully so it wouldn't roll off the back of my hand or soak into my sweater. I placed it on the tip of my index finger and held it up to the sun.

The beam of light that lit it through was a sign you were ok. I saw a fragment of your smile, a fraction of your eye.

I dropped anchor, sat cross-legged on the deck, and stored this new memory in your little pink box.

: :

Time for a round of battleships. I bomb your fleet at random. You sink my battleship. I torpedo your destroyer, but most of my shots end up in the water. You think it's hilarious, which winds me up a bit because I tend to be a sore loser. Still, I love how your laughter fills the air and settles back over us like a fine layer of snow.

A-8. Miss!

I love the sound of childhood in your voice, the pure melody you sing as you play at not yet being a grownup.

STANDING AT THE KITCHEN SINK, I would wonder about the scientific probability of the glass in my hand containing the same water that took you away. I'd hold it up to the light and stare at it, hoping to find a fragment of you.

Nothing. Dump it in the sink. Fill the glass again. Repeat.

Sometimes I'd spot a flicker of you among the suspended particles, hidden between the very molecules. You only appeared in fragments, like an image in a glittering nursery mobile of reflective shards. The tip of an ear, a scrap of bathing suit, the skin of your forearm. The good ones went into a sealed jar. Every drop a message from you. I had written your name on a piece of paper and taped it to the jar. Dancing, spinning images creating a segmented, kaleidoscopic carrousel version of you.

THAT DAY.

I recall your flippers weren't where they should have been in the closet. We looked for them everywhere, in the shed, in the garage, by the pool.

Eventually we gave up, climbed into the car, and headed for the beach.

The beach was fine amber sand and crowded with pasty people. They were playing catch, throwing frisbees, laying in the sun, running all over the place.

You had ambled off with your pail and shovel. I was stretched out next to your mother on a towel. You were playing in the shallow water, the tiny waves licking your toes, laughing as you threw sand at a shirtless boy who ran by. You were laughing. You were laughing so hard you strained your vocal chords. Laughing yourself hoarse.

Then it stopped. Your laughter just evaporated, and you were gone.

I thought I spotted you about a hundred yards off, between two foaming swells. You seemed to be fighting the waves, struggling for air. Then you went under and never came up.

A grenade went off inside me. My blood turned black.

I ran to you, the sand scorching my feet, my lungs bursting for air. I ran to you, but you were gone forever.

They called in the coast guard, professional divers, nuclear submarines. They didn't find you. The next day, on page 7, they ran something about a tragic accident, a momentary distraction with fatal consequences.

::

The drive home without you that night was horrific. Absolute silence. My hands like claws on the steering wheel, your mother's head leaning against the window.

I kept adjusting the rearview mirror, but your empty booster seat stayed smack in the centre of my field of vision.

Enough. Stop. Engine still running. Get out. Give the seat a time out in the trunk.

My head hollow, water in my ears, the world spinning. Knees biting into the gravel, tears flooding the roadside. Mom got out, and we stayed there for a long time, clinging to each other. Still not grasping the enormity of what had happened.

Back home the seat went in the shed with your hula hoop and roller skates, between the propane tank and the lawnmower.

That first night without you my heart stopped beating more than once. We couldn't sleep. Despite the exhaustion, despite the desire to wake up from this nightmare. When the sun came up, you weren't there.

::

Our house was an impregnable fortress with ramparts and a drawbridge, partly hidden behind a row of big evergreens amassing snow on their branches. I would put up wooden fences around the smaller ones to help them get through the winter.

There was a hammock strung up in the porch. A woodpile, a wind chime, and a greenhouse where your mother grew herbs and different varieties of rare orchids.

Our home smelled of camphor, wood smoke, and green tea. The flowerbeds in the backyard were bursting with bright coloured flowers and perennials.

There was a swing, a sandbox, and even a wading pool. I had imported parts of the Galapagos to our yard for you. Fire-breathing iguanas, ancient turtles, greyish green-scaled pangolins. You had spread eggshells along the footpath, and they cracked underfoot. We could hear the creatures living in the garden coming long before we could see them through the picture window. A few times we spotted giant salamanders almost six feet long, speckled newts, bright coloured insects.

::

After you disappeared, the house we lived in was just too big. It creaked and moaned at night, mourning the cruel lack of warmth.

Our home had suddenly grown into a cold expanse, as if winter had swallowed up the rest of the year.

We lived in a house that didn't want us anymore.

::

I'd become a prisoner to the constant sound of waves. The rush of water drowned out everything else. I could no longer hear the birds in the morning or cicadas in the afternoon. I was sure there was a stream running somewhere, maybe under the floorboards. I tore them up, one by one, but couldn't find the source of the sound filling my ears.

I was scared. I was cold right down to my bones. I lost weight. Time kept passing without slowing down, and I tried to ignore it by reliving the same old memories.

Upstairs, I paced the hallway outside your room. I wrapped myself in your scent and rocked your little ghost to sleep.

No news of you in 12 days.

::

Total silence. No stars except a tiny pulsar twinkling in the great dome of the sky.

I like to wake at dawn and contemplate the pinks and purples as they sway soundlessly over the deep shades of blue.

I like the glassy, unruffled feel of quiet mornings.

Naked, placid silence slipping into a turbid daybreak. I revisit the places we used to go together: the zoo, the woods where we would camp out in the summer, the park near the ice cream store, the local pet shop, the cottage, the sandy beach.

DID I EVER TELL YOU how I met your mother? It was at a housewarming party on a dusky August evening. Some mutual friends celebrating a new home, a new life. Neither of us knew anyone else there.

The usual small talk about the weather and work. About math, finance, and our shared aversion to instant rice and bland people. She loved hanging gardens, I couldn't get enough of astronomy and had a thing for rainy days.

We ended up on the couch, caught up in whispers and giggles. Our conversation went on forever and echoed into eternity.

She was a silent screen star, with dark hair and curly eyelashes. Her birthday was October 12. She talked in her sleep. She liked tapioca pudding, Indian food, and thick wool sweaters. Her mouth was a work of art.

She used to say, "Your face is making me dizzy," and send me out for a walk while she vacuumed. She kicked me out like that every Sunday morning so she could clean the house. Your mother hated dust and couldn't stand breadcrumbs on the counter.

In the summer, she would squeeze lemons by the hundred to make lemonade. Fall was soup season, and every day brought with it the fragrance of a different vegetable. In winter she would light cinnamon-scented candles and put them by the window.

::

After you were gone, we would sit together in the living room after work. Every day her eyes would spill over with a new wave of sorrow I was powerless to stem.

Every night we would cling to each other on the couch until we fell asleep.

::

Most nights I cried while doing the dishes. Soundlessly, but I couldn't keep my shoulders from shaking. I told myself it was a good thing, that it would release all the water weighing me down inside, pushing against my lungs, making every movement feel like torture. It was a foggy, indefinable feeling, like when you've overslept or when you think you might have forgotten to turn off the lights when you went out.

Since every single drop of water is inter-connected, I started searching for you in the mist of November evenings and in puddles on city sidewalks. I screamed your name into toilet bowls and the kitchen sink. Called out to you for hours on end, praying your little voice would answer.

::

Mommy cried a lot, too. At night her chest heaved in wretched sighs. Very gently, so she wouldn't wake, I would slide a hand between her ribs to cradle her heart in my palm, hoping it would soothe her a little.

She spent a lot of time in the bathtub. She would immerse herself completely, staying underwater and holding her breath as long as she could, depriving herself of air until she came up gasping. I watched her in silence.

::

I walked up behind her one day to plant a comforting kiss on the side of her neck. The instant my lips made contact, I felt a sharp zap. I jumped back, stunned by the electrical charge she gave off.

From that moment on, I tried to avoid touching her. I was scared to hug her or even get too close to her. I was afraid of the rumbling inside her and the great storm raging between us.

She would lock herself in the greenhouse and play music loud enough to cover the sound of her sobs.

She couldn't stand the sound of the kitchen clock anymore. She said she couldn't bear to hear the seconds tick away.

For me it was like living through a drought. I was like a bad tooth to her, a splinter under her nail, a foreign body in a wound.

I didn't know what else to do but spend all day in the living room, looking out the window, staring at the TV, or sleeping on the couch, with no idea how to move forward.

Marie accused me of not caring. She hated that we didn't talk anymore, she hated the lack of affection between us. She was angry at me for spending hours slumped in the armchair where I kept watch night and day. I tried to focus on her words, but it was a struggle: there was a constant, nagging gurgling in my ears. It was coming from the walls this time.

TODAY IS LADYBUG DAY. It's a holiday. There's space on my lap for you to sit. I'm in the Tyrrhenian Sea, and a cloud of little yellow, red, and black beetles has invaded the mainsail, jib, and guy lines.

Remember the time we got home and the walls were covered in ladybugs? It was a beautiful, bright blue day and the ladybugs were out sunning their wings on the front of the house. Hundreds of thousands of them. Love was in the air, the lilacs were blooming, and your mother and I could still talk for hours. I would tuck you into bed once the sun went down. I remember rolling around on the lawn with you in the backyard. The sweet murmur of your breath against my cheek. Back then I still held your hand to cross the street.

::

Deprived of you, your mother was a gathering storm. She stopped coming to see me on the couch when she got home. She would throw open the door and toss her keys on the kitchen counter. I'd become a tourist in my own life, a pillar of salt commemorating the lost.

I continued to wander around the house in a fog. My big, gnarled hands hanging limp against my thighs. The trickling sound of water in my head had become a gushing torrent.

Outside, a blizzard had been blowing forever.

::

Your coffin is buried in a quiet place overlooking the St. Lawrence River. There's a headstone with your name on it and colourful flowers whose petals collect rainwater where squirrels and muskrats come to drink.

Your mom would ask me to drive her to the cemetery at least twice a week.

She would carefully remove the dead flower-heads and pull up the dandelions around your headstone. She always brought a big blanket to spread out over your grave. Laying there on her side, she looked like she could have stayed forever. She would sob, clenching tufts of grass, clawing the earth to sow kisses, laying to rest all her regrets and hopes in one long, inaudible lament. I would wait in the car. I couldn't understand why she did it, because I knew you weren't there.

When the daylight began to wane, I'd honk the horn or walk down to get her.

Back home she would bolt upstairs to burrow under the blankets, unwashed and in her clothes. Dirty tissues in her cardigan pockets, stringy hair, a muddy trail of grimy fingermarks in the hallway. I would spend hours scrubbing the walls, but the stains never really went away.

::

The noise coming from inside the walls became clearer and more insistent over time. It nagged at me, a furtive slithering sound. Like something alive and crawling.

Your mom often came downstairs to see me at night. She'd seem surprised to see me with my ear to the wall, shushing her with a finger. She'd beg me to come to bed. I'd nod then stay put, attentive to even the slightest movement.

41

I tried bringing it up with her more than once, but she insisted she didn't know what I was talking about. She refused to acknowledge the awful grinding sound. She wouldn't listen. She wouldn't help me find where it was coming from. All she wanted to do was look after her plants.

I tried to fill the silence between us, but it was impossible. I had no words left for her.

THE MILKY WAY looks like an enormous swarm of krill. They both glow in the dark. I sail all night over a thick, green phosphorous cloud, humming tunes just for you. I carefully bait my lines as the great cluster of our galaxy disappears to make way for a sun that bursts from the sea, turning the water a coppery gold.

Just before I fall asleep I sometimes talk to you as if you were floating right next to me. The occasional comet comes to keep me company, streaking light across the black night sky.

You are a breath on my neck, a gentle wind drawing me further out to sea. You're a rain shower released inside me. I spin the memory of you into long cords and wrap them around myself like a cloak.

Every day is the day you died. Every morning the sound of water drags me awake, and I lie listening in terror for minutes on end. I've combed the Nile and probed the Mediterranean and South China seas without finding any trace of you.

Some fishermen on the Amazon said they'd seen you swimming with manatees. They recognized the string of pearls around your neck. The necklace with the little daisies your mom and I bought at the shopping mall.

I managed to net a sea serpent over four feet long. It bled pale yellow and covered the deck. After days without food, I tore into the flesh with my teeth. It was crawling with worms and made me sick.

::

One day I noticed the plaster in a corner of the living room had swelled. I carefully ran my fingers over the eggshell cracks in the paint and kept a close watch on that corner for a while.

Marie got angry at me, muttering something incomprehensible about needing to get away. I could see her lips moving, but I couldn't make out the words that came out of her mouth.

I couldn't concentrate on what she was saying. The surge of the waves filled the hollow space inside me, a languorous rhythm that weighed me down like a sleeping pill or a sad song.

She said she couldn't stand living in our house anymore. She said it felt like you were everywhere. In every corner, every recess, in places she had forgotten even existed. Places you still haunted without meaning to.

She talked about a fresh start, a new life, helping each other heal. She begged me to hold her in my arms.

I checked the living room every morning as a precaution. Carefully, so as not to wake your mother, I would pull the furniture away from the walls and examine the plaster with my fingertips, searching for the slightest sign: a hole or crack. The ceiling needed inspecting too. I would hold an ear to it to check for any sign of movement. The crack in the corner kept getting bigger.

Your mom kept threatening to quit her job. I couldn't remember the last time I'd been to work.

::

A permanent state of tranquility had settled over the entire house. If I held my breath long enough and calmed my beating heart, I could even hear the snowflakes landing on the sidewalk.

When I closed my eyes, I could feel the changing seasons on my skin. The anxious quiver of melting snow, the sound of sunlight spreading over the house across the street, the clouds slipping across the sky. I learned their shapes and names by heart.

::

I must have spent a century in that latent state, season after season while the sun gradually crept over the wall of the house across the street.

I should have drowned too. I should have jumped in and stretched out my fingers to grab your hand. And now we are separated by gallons of water, my baby girl.

Your mother and I went under that day too. If only words had managed to fill the void between us. If only words could have broken the silence, maybe we could have saved whatever was left of us.

Gradually the shine faded from everything. There was rust around the bathtub drain. Soup-making season faded to a steady grey drizzle, then to flu season. Even words were losing ground. Marie and I rarely spoke and when we did it was about the shopping list or how we needed to mow the lawn again already.

Gradually the silence became a shrill, undeniable reality, like a whistling kettle or tires squealing on a wet road. Never could I have imagined such torture, such relentless hammering. Never could I have believed that the passage of time could become such a terrible thing.

I smashed the old clock in the kitchen because I couldn't stand to hear Marie complain about the seconds ticking by.

LYING IN MY BUNK, I examine my memories of you in the dark, brushing against them with my eyelashes. And sometimes I hear the sound of eggshells cracking. I rush up on deck, scanning the shadows, hoping for a glimpse of you, imagining myself sweeping you up in my arms, whispering that everything's ok, that Daddy's got you.

I understood now what your mother meant by the cold that had us in its grip. The silence was driving me crazy.

I had started arguing with my reflection in the bathroom mirror, screaming at it for hours, driving each syllable home with a fist.

I couldn't really remember your funeral. Had I even gone? Yes, I had. I remember shaking a procession of hands. A little white coffin.

Whimpering aunts and a parade of impeccable shoes. I remember the buffet of cheese sandwiches and warm potato salad.

No one had warned us about the bitter cold, the great void.

How can a catastrophe like ours fail to sway the tides, shift the Earth on its axis, or send the stock market crashing?

::

One day as I was walking past a fish shop I got an idea. I brought home four live rainbow trout. At $3.95 apiece it seemed like a bargain.

I went straight home and waited for your mom in the kitchen with my surprise. I decided to fill the huge porcelain sink with water and keep the fish in there.

The streetlights were on and it was dark out by the time she came home. I must have been lost in my thoughts. When she saw the fish sloshing around in the sink, she screamed. It wasn't the reaction I'd expected. She flat-out refused when I suggested we wash the dishes in the bathtub, and she didn't want to put the fish in the bathroom either.

She said we should just eat them.

I stormed off to the bedroom in disgust, slammed the door behind me, and threw myself at the bed, snatching away the blankets to grab a pillow. Then I marched back to the kitchen with a pillowcase and dropped the frantic trout in there one by one.

It was freezing outside and the streets were covered in salt. I walked around until it felt like my bone marrow had turned to ice.

I held the fish safe and warm under my coat and spoke to them softly. Fortunately the walk soothed them, and soon they were sleeping like babies.

By that point I was numb and in a daze. I wandered over to the park, figuring it would be empty at that hour.

Other people's kids had been in bed for hours, and it was too cold for the usual gaggle of teen-agers to be outside.

The swings were motionless and the slide was half buried in snow. I put my pillowcase down on a bench and dug a hole in the snow with my hands.

I gently laid the trout in there and promised to come back for them in the spring. Then I covered them up and marked the spot with a piece of wood.

When I came back, they had spawned.

: :

One day I was watching a stratus with ragged edges slowly glide across the sky, too focused to notice the sun going down. By the time I roused myself from my daydreams, I was half hidden in darkness. Your mother came up the stairs. I lay on the living-room floor and played dead.

She stormed into the room, snatched the jar from my hands, and downed it in one go. Can you believe it? She drank the water in my jar! Every fragment of you I'd spent months collecting. First the fish, now this. She'd gone too far. I pulled myself to my feet, seething and shouting.

She looked at me with surprise, then pity.

She threw herself at me, pummeling my chest, yelling, bawling, sniffling, her tears soaking into my sleeves.

I didn't want her to leave. You have to believe me.

But eventually she calmed down. She cleared her throat, dried her eyes on her sleeves, and started gathering her things together. Just a few books and some clothes. She packed it all into the beige carry-on case, the one we used to keep in our bedroom closet, where we used to hide your Christmas presents and Easter chocolates.

We had only very brief contact after that. From then on I would live alone. She opened the door, and I could hear her footsteps fading away down the path of broken shells.

::

Your mother had been gone for days, maybe months. There was hardly anything left of her in the house, nothing at all of you.

I wandered from room to room like a lunatic. The bed unmade. Nothing to eat.

I was sick of looking out the same window. Sick of white walls. Sick of the ice-covered ground.

As luck would have it, the hardware store was still open.

I ran over and bought eight sandbags.

Back home, with the sandbags in a neat pile, I removed all the furniture from the living room.

The TV and bookcase went into the bedroom. I managed to drag the couch and coffee table into the next room.

I slashed open each bag in turn on the living-room floor and spread the sand out evenly with my hands. Then I sat against the wall and rested my hands on my knees. I could really hear the water now. I could hear the ocean. The far wall slowly faded away as the sea spread toward me in a series of gentle waves, lapping at my toes. The ceiling collapsed and I threw open the windows and let in the sterns and the cormorants.

I could feel the salty sea breeze against my face and bare arms.

I made a beach where I could spend all day building sand castles the tide could never destroy. A beach far from the predatory sea and pestering gulls, a warm place to sleep at night.

At an antique shop I found a paper lantern patterned with multicoloured fish and shells that projected a rainbow of marine life on the walls. Little fish making funny faces. A starfish and a friendly crab. A winking seahorse. You would have loved it.

::

The plum tree in the yard kept blossoming despite my chronic negligence. The fruit grew plump, ripened, and rotted. Growing, ripening, and rotting, faster and faster, until it all happened in the blink of an eye.

One morning I poured my millionth, or perhaps my ten millionth, glass of water and held it up to the light, searching for a fragment of you, as always. And suddenly I knew.

I knew my redemption lay out at sea, with you. It made perfect sense. All bodies of water are drawn to the sea. That's where your body had to be. It couldn't be otherwise.

It was like a great flash of light in my darkness, a revelation that made me smile despite my sagging shoulders.

Down at the port I paced the docks and floating piers in slow, deliberate steps. The day was flooded with dogged yellow light that seemed to emanate from everywhere at once. It was the kind of summer day where the humidity hits you in merciless waves.

I spent a long time watching an old sailor working on his boat. He was patching a hole in the hull with strips of fiberglass. I said hello, and we talked for a while.

He'd been sailing his whole life, and he understood the whims of the sea. Very patiently he explained how to build a sailboat sturdy enough to track you down. Which materials to use, how to build a frame and apply fiberglass. Over the months that followed, he invited me aboard and taught me to sail. How to navigate, tie sailing knots, and even find my way using the stars.

I built the boat right out on the front lawn, tools and materials scattered everywhere, working day and night much to the annoyance of the neighbours, who constantly complained about all the noise and cursing.

::

I was curious to find out why your mom used to hold her breath in the bathtub, back when we were still living together. So I fetched the big bucket from the garage, the one we'd use to wash the car, and filled it with water. I took a slight breath, and went in face first up to my neck.

Minutes passed as my entire body revolted against the lack of oxygen and went into spasms, feet kicking at the garage floor, knuckles scraping against the edge of the bucket. That's when I understood what she had been subjecting herself to on a regular basis. The nausea, the panic, the sheer terror.

When I finally pulled my head out, the neighbours were standing there on the sidewalk, looking stunned.

I hadn't realized I'd left the garage door open.

::

Someone was at the front door, banging and calling my name. Keys jingling. I eyed the street through the curtains, then pulled my shirt off, rolled it up, and jammed it under the door.

I bolted into the bedroom and hid behind the mattress that was leaning against the wall.

Marie came in. She went room to room calling my name until she found me sandwiched between the heater and our double mattress.

I was surprised by how much she had changed. She had cut her hair short and lost a lot of weight. She seemed calm and composed. Smiling like she was happy to see me. She didn't appear to recognize me right away. Perhaps because I was gaunt and grimy, grey-haired, bearded, and barefoot.

Seeing her again after all that time apart, part of me wondered whether I could have tried harder to keep her near, to unite our two solitudes, to come together.

I tried to put my hand on her shoulder, but my fingers on her skin brought an instant shock. She shook her head, picked up her mail, and left.

::

I'm out of paper. On deck now, setting your name down with squid ink and compass tip until it covers my skin. A vision of these tattoos melting under the noonday sun, ink streaming over the deck and into the vast ocean to find you. My ink surrounding you, forming a shield against predators, a break against groundswells, then a ladder, then a net. All the way back to me.

::

I navigated a smack of stinging jellyfish, sailed the Strait of Malacca surrounded by giant manta rays, battled Somali pirates and Ottoman corsairs. I crossed paths with a school of bluefin tuna and eventually managed to spear one with a gaff hook and scoop it up.

You should have seen me fight that thing. An absolute beast. The size of it. As big around as I am. A magnificent fish, but its raw flesh made me queasy for the rest of the day and much of the night.

No sign of you in 422 days.

::

The house was in shambles. The bathtub over-flowing. The living room had been transformed into a beach, where I spent most of my time. My supplies were running low, and I got by on raw eggs and soggy flour.

I built a new rudder and installed it on the kitchen island, threw open the windows to let in the breeze, took apart the table and chairs, gutted the couch, and stacked everything up against the wall to make more room.

::

Over the next few days, a network of veins spread across the walls and ceiling beneath the paint, growing until it completely covered the ground floor.

Then a leak sprung one morning and the water started seeping in. I patched it with duct tape and a cushion from the sofa. The din kept getting louder by the day, rumbling constantly and rattling the windows like a transport truck driving past.

A few days later the water burst a hole in the kitchen wall and flooded the living room with black water.

Leaks sprung all over the place, and I ran around trying to plug them. I was still sure I could put off the inevitable and save the house. I couldn't. Upstairs, the water was already encroaching into your pink bedroom. I wanted to take a few reminders of you, but the water was already everywhere, so I grabbed the first thing I saw: the little pink box on your bed. Then I fled. Everything I owned was tossed into a big canvas bag, and I ran straight to the port, blood pounding in my temples. I launched the boat myself and left the city behind, sailing all the way down the St. Lawrence to its mouth, where I joined the Gulf Stream.

I spotted a few tall ships. Massive, proud, majestic three-masters cutting through the water with ease.

I had good sea legs, there was no denying that, but my technical skills were cruelly lacking. I'd never piloted this type of craft alone before.

The salt bit into my skin, and the sun scorched my back, shoulders, and neck. My sails hopelessly tangled, my lines slack and dragging, the rudder with a mind of its own. But gradually I asserted myself as the one in charge of this vessel. You would have been proud of me. I was a captain. The same man who knew practically nothing about navigation. The same man who used to be terrified of the sea.

C-4. Hit!

: :

Did you know that in some very dry countries they string nets among the clouds in the mountaintops? The fog gets trapped in the nets, then trickles down to the villages below.

You're like one of those nets stretched out inside me.

::

"Look, Mom! Marbles!" Your voice reverberates inside me like the echo of a dream. I cling to those memories. They keep me alive. The wind was pounding against our bedroom window that night. You were afraid of the storm and climbed into bed with us and curled up against your mom.

"Marbles," you said, pointing out the window. She held you in her arms and told you we were safe in there, dry and warm. We stayed like that all night, together and sheltered from the storm outside.

::

Long strips of purplish clouds stretch over the deep, dark sky. Venus guides me over the waves. Pollux rises lamely, his twin Castor lagging behind.

I draw a hopscotch court on deck with the chalk of my bones. It runs from heaven to hell. I fish around in my canvas bag and find a pair of ivory dice. I roll a six.

You roll a four and sing as you hop. I smile. I'm beaming. My boat remains motionless, surrounded by endless water.

::

Yo ho and a bottle of rum! Another windless day. The sea is flat. My nets lay empty in the water.

At night I sail to the phosphorescent glow of multicoloured octopus and raw moonlight. The sound of turtle eggs hatching on the deck.

Come here, babygirl. It's time to go home.

D-9. Hit and sunk!

YOU USED TO HAVE NIGHT TERRORS. You'd wake up screaming, thrashing around. Even together we couldn't hold you down. You'd be beside yourself, speaking in tongues, howling like a wolf. When you finally calmed down, you'd crawl into bed with us. Your skin against mine, mine against your mother's, you'd fall asleep again.

::

Did you know that Saturn's mass is so low it would float if you dropped it in water?

Did you know its rings are made of rock and ice? The same kind of ice besieging my boat. The same ice you, me, and Mom used to skate on every winter in the park. When Grandpa died, I told you he'd been a famous speed skater and that now he was zipping around Saturn on the biggest skating rink in the universe.

Every night for months we watched the night sky through my telescope. I'd tell you to look for a tiny shadow speeding past Saturn. You would concentrate really hard and quietly fall asleep on my lap without spotting him.

There are a thousand constellations of you still inside me. Your name runs into every memory and colours every thought.

::

I'm ok. I devoured that bird with a pinch of salt and some mollusks that were clinging to the hull. The sun bleeds into the ocean, staining the water glossy red and black. I'm ok.

My sails are trimmed and I'm clipping along.

A thick fog rises and drowns my whole boat. It's so dense I can hardly keep going. Hard to tell where the sky ends and the sea begins. I drop anchor and wait for it to lift.

::

Remember that kid at school who said girls couldn't run as fast as boys? You wanted to show him. You wanted to shut him up. You set out to beat him in an impromptu schoolyard race. You ended up having a pretty bad asthma attack, and Mom had to pick you up at the nurse's station at lunchtime.

That night I brought you back a moonstone from the shopping mall.

: :

What do you know about the origins of the moon, sweetie? One theory is that the Earth and the moon formed simultaneously from the same elements and dust particles. Part of the same equation, like you and me.

If I had known you'd be with us for such a short time, I would have kept you awake every moment of it. I would have fought sleep with everything I had. If we had to sleep, it would be together in your little bed. I should have watched when you jumped off the highest diving board at the swimming pool or when you went down the big slide at the park. If I'd known, I would really have watched, instead of pretending to, instead of chatting to someone about the weather.

THE SKY IS CLEAR, but thunder rumbles in the distance. The sea is tense. A shudder runs through the water.

Thousands of flying fish break the surface and glide through the air on each side of my boat, their silver bodies reflecting sunlight like tiny flashes of heat.

You are dancing among the waves, playing hide-and-seek between the currents. But I see you. You peek out from behind piles of seafoam. You slip under the hull. I count to one hundred.

There's a storm about three or four days off. My maps are laid out flat in front of me, marking narrow passages and water depths. They're covered in numbers and equations I have to decipher to plot a safe course all the way to you. Finally.

THAT DAY.

I seem to recall you'd lost your right shoe. We searched for a while, then forgot about it and went for a swim in the lake behind the cottage. I couldn't find your orange water wings either, but I figured it didn't matter because I'd be keeping an eye on you anyway. I told you to wait while I built a fire in the firepit. You were sitting on the dock, dangling your feet in the water, giggling.

I looked away for barely a second. I bent over to pick up some wood, and when I looked up, you were gone. You weren't hiding behind the row of trees that ran alongside the cottage. The treehouse was empty. I called your name.

I looked under the porch, in the attic, in the basement. I felt nauseous. I felt the world coming to an end. I lost my mind. I screamed your name. It rang in my ears for hours.

When the police questioned me, they accused me of neglect, of leaving you unsupervised. They blamed me for your disappearance.

The next day we were just a line or two in the local paper. A tragic accident, a momentary distraction with fatal consequences.

I'M MOVING AT A GOOD CLIP, tacking left and right. My whole body beaten by the merciless winds of Cape Horn, bones bent, gripping the fishing nets and bits of string holding my sailboat together. The storm arrives with unimaginable violence. It pounds my face, lacerates my numb hands, and throws me in every possible direction. But it won't beat me. I won't let it.

Slowly but surely my boat begins to right itself. My hands are rock solid. Nothing is going to stop me. I'm a leaden monolith. Stable as a reef. Nothing can push me back.

::

Did you know the Great Red Spot on Jupiter is actually a giant storm in a perpetual spin? It's big enough to hold two or three Earth-sized planets.

Did you know the surface of Mercury is a roiling carpet of dust blown around by solar winds? Did you know the light from a dead star can still be seen long after it has gone out?

THAT DAY.

I swear, I tried. I tried everything. Our fingertips brushed together. I grabbed you by the forearm, but the current was too strong, and you were being pulled down too fast. I swear by your name engraved on my skin. On the head of my dead bird.

I can't even swim, but there I was, swallowing water by the bucketful, spitting, coughing, desperate to get back to shore, howling your name. Cramped, gasping, and spent. Spitting up saliva and snot and despair. Someone pulled me out. Without you.

I had become a momentary distraction with fatal consequences, a tragic accident.

::

I set out to find you. Sailing over black and purple waves, working the bilge pump to keep afloat. I'm almost there, sweetie. Lead me to you. Send a narwhal or humpback whale to guide me. Daddy's cold and hungry, but he's still here. I've lashed myself to the wheel. I sleep standing up. I'll keep sailing day and night until I reach you.

::

The sea can't hurt me anymore. It's already taken everything. Redemption lies somewhere in a seahorse cemetery, deep in a cave, or on the side of an underwater mountain. Somewhere close to you.

Blasted by the cruel storm, sailing blind, dodging reefs, shaken by violent winds that smell of Armageddon. If I make it through this cyclone I'll be free. Free from the sea. Free from Marie. I can't decide which is more beautiful, Marie or the sea.

I rinse my mouth with seawater to purge the taste of metal. It tastes like blood, or fear. Or canned tuna. I can't tell which.

::

Tattered sails, broken mast, warped rudder. The final leg of this journey. It's time to go.

I take my pocketknife and carve my name into the rotted wood of the mast, knowing it's of absolutely no importance.

I want to leave a trace of my passage, however slight. Without a marked grave, who will know I ever existed?

I fill my slicker pockets with your moonstones to hasten our reunion.

I slide slowly into the water, clinging to the guardrail. I fill my lungs and abandon my boat to the raging storm.

I'll drift down to the seabed and join all the souls lost at sea, and I'll swim forever among seaweed and plankton, rocked by a medusan lullaby.

Crabs will pick clean my bones, the sea inherit my decrepit ship.

Below, the phantom glow of spectral cephalopods leads me to you. You touch my face, rest your hands on my chest.

Your soles settle into my palms like the undoing of continental drift, and I bind us together with 50 fathoms of strong cable.

There you are, floating over an emerald reef.

Whole again now, my arms around you, spinning like ballroom dancers, plunging into clear infinity.

Anchoring you, buoyed by you.

I'll never take my eyes off you again.

QC Fiction brings you the very best of a new generation of Quebec storytellers, sharing surprising, interesting novels in flawless English translation.

Available from QC Fiction:

Visit **qcfiction.com** for details and to subscribe to a full season of QC Fiction titles.

Printed by Imprimerie Gauvin
Gatineau, Québec